DIARY OF A WIMPY KID

DIARY
of a
Wimpy Kid

THE LAST STRAW

by Jeff Kinney

PUFFIN

PUFFIN BOOKS

Published by the Penguin Group
Penguin Books Ltd, 80 Strand, London WC2R 0RL, England
Penguin Group (USA) Inc., 375 Hudson Street, New York, New York 10014, USA
Penguin Group (Canada), 90 Eglinton Avenue East, Suite 700, Toronto, Ontario, Canada M4P 2Y3
(a division of Pearson Penguin Canada Inc.)
Penguin Ireland, 25 St Stephen's Green, Dublin 2, Ireland (a division of Penguin Books Ltd)
Penguin Group (Australia), 250 Camberwell Road, Camberwell, Victoria 3124, Australia
(a division of Pearson Australia Group Pty Ltd)
Penguin Books India Pvt Ltd, 11 Community Centre, Panchsheel Park, New Delhi – 110 017, India
Penguin Group (NZ), 67 Apollo Drive, Rosedale, North Shore 0632, New Zealand
(a division of Pearson New Zealand Ltd)
Penguin Books (South Africa) (Pty) Ltd, 24 Sturdee Avenue, Rosebank,
Johannesburg 2196, South Africa

Penguin Books Ltd, Registered Offices: 80 Strand, London WC2R 0RL, England

puffinbooks.com

First published in the English language in 2009
by Harry N. Abrams, Incorporated, New York
(All rights reserved in all countries by Harry N. Abrams, Inc.)
Published in Great Britain in Puffin Books 2009

001

Copyright © Jeff Kinney, 2009
All rights reserved

British Library Cataloguing in Publication Data
A CIP catalogue record for this book is available from the British Library

ISBN: 978-0-241-33573-4

www.greenpenguin.co.uk

TO TIM

New Year's Day

You know how you're supposed to come up with a list of "resolutions" at the beginning of the year to try to make yourself a better person?

Well, the problem is it's not easy for me to think of ways to improve myself, because I'm already pretty much one of the best people I know.

So this year my resolution is to try to help OTHER people improve. But the thing I'm finding out is that some people don't really appreciate it when you're trying to be helpful.

One thing I noticed right off the bat is that the people in my family are doing a lousy job sticking to THEIR New Year's resolutions.

Mom said she was gonna start going to the gym today, but she spent the whole afternoon watching TV.

And Dad said he was gonna go on a strict diet, but after dinner I caught him out in the garage, stuffing his face with brownies.

Even my little brother, Manny, couldn't stick with his resolution.

This morning he told everyone that he's a "big boy" and he's giving up his pacifier for good. Then he threw his favourite binkie in the trash.

Well, THAT New Year's resolution didn't even last a full MINUTE.

The only person in my family who didn't come up with a resolution is my older brother, Rodrick, and that's a pity because his list should be about a mile and a half long.

3

So I decided to come up with a programme to help Rodrick be a better person. I called my plan "Three Strikes and You're Out". The basic idea was that every time I saw Rodrick messing up, I'd mark a little "X" on his chart.

Well, Rodrick got all three strikes before I even had a chance to decide what "You're Out" meant.

Anyway, I'm starting to wonder if I should just bag MY resolution, too. It's a lot of work, and so far I haven't really made any progress.

Besides, after I reminded Mom for like the billionth time to stop chewing her crisps so loud, she made a really good point. She said, "Everyone can't be as perfect as YOU, Gregory." And from what I've seen so far I think she's right.

Thursday

Dad is giving this diet thing another try, and that's bad news for me. He's gone about three days without eating any chocolate, and he's been SUPER cranky.

The other day, after Dad woke me up and told me to get ready for school, I accidentally fell back asleep. Believe me, that's the last time I'll make THAT mistake.

Part of the problem is that Dad always wakes me up before Mom's out of the shower, so I know that I still have like ten more minutes before I need to get out of bed for real.

Yesterday I came up with a pretty good way to get some extra sleep time without making Dad mad. After he woke me up, I took all of my blankets down the hall with me and waited outside the bathroom for my turn in the shower.

Then I lay down right on top of the heater vent. And when the furnace was blowing, the experience was even BETTER than being in bed.

The problem was the heat only stayed on for about five minutes at a time. So when the furnace wasn't running, I was just lying there on this cold piece of metal.

This morning, while I was waiting for Mom to be done with her shower, I remembered someone gave her a bathrobe for Christmas. So I went into her closet and got it.

Let me just say that was one of the smartest moves I've ever made. Wearing that thing was like being wrapped in a big, fluffy towel that just came out of the dryer.

In fact, I liked it so much, I even wore it AFTER my shower. I think Dad might've been jealous HE didn't come up with the robe idea first, because when I came to the kitchen table, he seemed extra grumpy.

I tell you, women have the right idea with this bathrobe thing. Now I'm wondering what ELSE I'm missing out on.

I just wish I had asked for my own bathrobe for Christmas, because I'm sure Mom is gonna make me give hers back.

I struck out on gifts again this year. I knew I was in for a rough day when I came downstairs on Christmas morning and the only presents in my stocking were a stick of deodorant and a "travel dictionary".

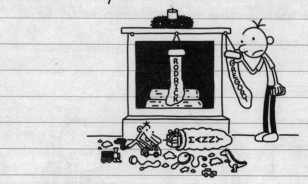

I guess once you're in middle school, grown-ups decide you're too old for toys or anything that's actually fun.

But then they still expect you to be all excited when you open the lame gifts they get you.

Most of my gifts this year were books or clothes. The closest thing I got to a toy was a present from Uncle Charlie.

When I unwrapped Uncle Charlie's gift, I didn't even know what it was supposed to be. It was this big plastic ring with a net attached to it.

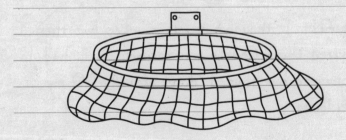

Uncle Charlie explained that it was a "Laundry Hoop" for my bedroom. He said I was supposed to hang the Laundry Hoop on the back of my door and it would make putting away my dirty clothes "fun".

At first I thought it was a joke, but then I realized Uncle Charlie was serious. So I had to explain to him that I don't actually DO my own laundry.

I told him I just throw my dirty clothes on the floor, and Mom picks them up and takes them downstairs to the laundry room.

Then, a few days later, everything comes back to me in nice, folded piles.

I told Uncle Charlie he should just return the Laundry Hoop and give me cash so I could buy something I'd actually USE.

That's when Mom spoke up. She told Uncle Charlie she thought the Laundry Hoop was a GREAT idea.

Then she said that from now on I'd be doing my OWN laundry. So, basically, it ends up that Uncle Charlie got me a chore for Christmas.

It really stinks that I got such crummy gifts this year. I put in a lot of effort buttering people up for the past few months, and I thought it would pay off on Christmas.

Now that I'm responsible for my own laundry, I guess I'm kind of GLAD I got a bunch of clothes. I might actually make it through the whole school year before I run out of clean stuff to wear.

Monday

When me and Rowley got to our bus stop today, we found a nasty surprise. There was a piece of paper taped to our street sign, and it said that, effective today, our bus route was "rezoned". And what that means is now we have to WALK to school.

Well, I'd like to talk to the genius who came up with THAT idea, because our street is almost a quarter of a mile from the school.

Me and Rowley had to run to make it to school on time today. And what REALLY stunk was when our regular bus passed us by and it was full of kids from Whirley Street, the neighbourhood right next to ours.

The Whirley Street kids made monkey noises when they passed us, which was really annoying because that's exactly what WE used to do when we passed THEM.

I'll tell you one reason it's a bad idea to make kids walk to school. These days, teachers give you so much homework that, with all the books and papers you have to carry home, your backpack ends up weighing like a hundred pounds.

And, if you want to see what kind of an effect that has on kids over time, all you have to do is look at Rodrick and some of his friends.

Speaking of teenagers, Dad scored a pretty big victory today. The baddest teenager in our neighbourhood is this kid named Lenwood Heath, and he's kind of like Dad's arch-enemy. Dad has probably called the cops on Lenwood Heath about fifty times.

I guess Lenwood's parents got sick of his act, because they sent him off to military academy.

You'd think that would've made Dad pretty happy, but I don't think he'll be satisfied until every teenager on the planet gets sent off to juvenile hall or Alcatraz or something. And that includes Rodrick.

Yesterday Mom and Dad gave Rodrick some money to buy books so he could study for the SATs, but Rodrick spent the money on a tattoo instead.

I've still got a little time before I turn into a teenager. But the minute I do I guarantee you Dad will be looking for the first chance to ship me out.

Monday
For the past week or so, Manny has been getting out of bed every night and coming downstairs.

Instead of putting him right back to bed, Mom lets Manny sit with us and watch TV.

It's really not fair, because when Manny is with us I'm not allowed to watch any of the shows I like.

All I can say is when I was a kid there wasn't any of this "getting out of bed" stuff. I did it once or twice, but Dad put a stop to it real quick.

There was this book Dad used to read to me every night called "The Giving Tree". It was a really good book, but the back of it had a picture of the author, this guy named Shel Silverstein.

But Shel Silverstein looks more like a burglar or a pirate than a guy who should be writing books for kids.

Dad must have known that picture kind of freaked me out, because one night after I got out of bed, Dad said –

IF YOU GET OUT OF BED AGAIN TONIGHT, YOU'LL PROBABLY RUN INTO SHEL SILVERSTEIN IN THE HALLWAY.

That really did the trick. Ever since then, I STILL don't get out of bed at night, even if I really need to use the bathroom.

I don't think Mom and Dad read Manny any Shel Silverstein books, which probably explains why he keeps getting up after they put him to bed.

I've heard some of the stories Mom and Dad read to Manny, and let me just say that the people who write these books really have a racket going.

First of all, there are hardly any words in them, so I'm sure it only takes about five seconds to write one.

SILLY BEAR YAWNING, SILLY BEAR SAD.

SILLY BEAR SLEEPING, SILLY BEAR GLAD!

THE END.

I told Mom what I thought of Manny's books, and she said that if they were so easy to write, then I should try writing one myself.

So that's exactly what I did. Trust me, it wasn't hard, either. All you have to do is make up a character with a snappy name, and then make sure the character learns a lesson at the end of the book.

Now all I need to do is mail this thing off to a publisher and wait for the money to start rolling in.

Wise Up, Mr Shropsharp!

by Greg Heffley

Once upon a time there was this man named Mr Shropsharp who thought all these crazy thoughts.

One day Mr Shropsharp took a ride in his car.

But then...

And then…

MR SHROPSHARP, YOU WOULD HAVE DROWNED, BUT LUCKILY TOBUK HERE WAS SITTING ON AN ICEBERG, AND HE SAVED YOUR LIFE.

And so…

BEFORE, I SAID THAT POLAR BEARS ARE SOME USELESS ANIMALS, BUT NOW I CAN SEE THAT NOT EVERY POLAR BEAR IS SO USELESS AFTER ALL.

THE END

See what I mean? The only thing I noticed after I finished the book was that I forgot to make it rhyme. But the publisher is gonna have to pay me extra if they want THAT.

<u>Saturday</u>

Well, after spending the last two weeks walking to school, I was really looking forward to kicking back and doing nothing for two days.

The problem with watching TV on a Saturday is that the only thing that's on is bowling or golf. Plus, the sun comes through our sliding glass window, and you can barely see the TV screen anyway.

Today I wanted to change the channel, but the remote was on top of the coffee table. I was all comfortable, with my bowl of cereal in my lap, so I really didn't want to get up.

I tried using the Force to make the remote levitate to me, even though I've tried it a million times before and it's never worked once. Today I tried for about fifteen minutes and concentrated REALLY hard, but no luck. I just wish I'd known that Dad was standing right behind me the whole time.

Dad told me I was gonna have to go outside and get some exercise. I told Dad I exercise all the TIME and just this morning I used the bench press he got me.

But I should have come up with something more believable, because it was pretty obvious that wasn't true.

See, the reason Dad is on my case about exercise and all that is because he's got this boss named Mr Warren, and Mr Warren has three boys who are these crazy sports fanatics. Dad sees the Warren kids outside on their front lawn every day on his way home from work when his carpool goes by their house.

48...
49...
50!

So I think Dad is pretty disappointed every time he gets home and sees what HIS sons are up to.

Anyway, like I said, Dad kicked me out of the house today. I couldn't really think of anything I wanted to do, but then I had a good idea.

Yesterday at lunch, Albert Sandy was telling everyone about this guy in China or Thailand or someplace who could jump six feet straight up in the air, no joke. The way the guy did it was by digging a hole that was three inches deep and then jumping in and out of it a hundred times. The next day, the guy doubled the size of the hole, and he jumped in and out of THAT. By the fifth day, he was practically like a kangaroo.

Some of the guys at my table told Albert he was full of baloney, but what he was saying made a lot of sense to ME. Plus, I figured if I did what Albert said and then ADDED a few days to the programme all my problems with bullies could be over.

27

I got a shovel out of the garage and found a place in the front yard that looked like a good spot to dig. But before I could even get started, Mom came outside and asked me what I was up to.

I told Mom I was just digging a hole, but of course she didn't like THAT idea. So she came up with about twenty reasons why I wasn't allowed to do it.

Mom told me it was "dangerous" to dig in the yard because of underground electrical lines and sewage pipes and stuff. Then she made me promise up and down that I wouldn't dig any holes in our yard. So I promised.

Mom went inside, but then she kept watching me out of the window. I knew I was gonna have to take my shovel and go dig a hole somewhere else, so I headed up to Rowley's house.

I haven't been going up to Rowley's much lately, mostly because of Fregley. Fregley has been spending a lot of time in his front yard and, sure enough, that's where he was today.

DOES THIS SCAB SMELL FUNNY TO YOU?

My new strategy with Fregley is to just avoid eye contact and keep walking, and it seemed to do the trick today.

When I got to Rowley's, I told him my idea, and how the two of us would practically be ninjas if we stuck with this hole-jumping programme I'd planned out.

But Rowley didn't seem so hot on the idea. He said his parents might get mad if we dug a ten-foot hole in his front yard without asking them, so he was gonna have to get their permission first.

Now, if there's one thing I know about Rowley's parents, it's that they NEVER like my ideas. I told Rowley we could just cover the hole up with a tarp or a blanket or something and put some leaves on top of it, and his folks would never even find out. That seemed to convince him.

OK, so I admit that Rowley's parents might EVENTUALLY find out. But that wouldn't be for at least three or four months.

Me and Rowley found a good spot in the front yard to start digging, but we ran into a problem right away.

The ground was pretty much frozen SOLID, and we could hardly even make a dent.

I spent a few minutes trying before I handed the shovel over to Rowley. He couldn't really make any progress, either, but I gave him an extra-long turn so he could feel like he was contributing to the project.

Rowley got a little bit further than I did, but, when it started to get dark out, he gave up.

I guess we'll have to take another crack at this thing tomorrow.

Sunday
Well, I thought about it a lot overnight, and I realized that at the rate me and Rowley are going, we're gonna be in college before this hole is ten feet deep.

So I came up with a totally DIFFERENT idea for what we could do. I remembered this thing I saw on TV where scientists made a "time capsule" and filled it with a bunch of stuff like newspapers and DVDs and things like that. Then the scientists buried their time capsule in the ground. The idea was that in a few hundred years someone will come along and dig it up, and they can learn how people from our time used to live.

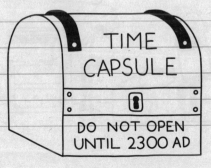

TIME
CAPSULE

DO NOT OPEN
UNTIL 2300 AD

I told Rowley about my idea, and he seemed pretty enthusiastic about it. Mostly, I think he was just glad we weren't gonna spend the next few years digging a hole.

I asked Rowley to donate some items to put in the time capsule, and that's when he got cold feet.

I told Rowley that if he put some of his Christmas presents in the time capsule, people in the future would get some really cool stuff when they opened the box. Rowley told me it wasn't fair, because I wasn't putting any of MY Christmas presents in the time capsule. So I had to explain to him that the people in the future would think we were really lame if they opened the box and it was filled with clothes and books.

Then I told Rowley I'd throw in three dollars of my OWN money to prove I was making sacrifices, too. That seemed to be enough to convince him to fork over one of his new video games and a couple of other things.

I actually had a secret plan that I wasn't letting Rowley in on. I knew that putting the cash in the time capsule was a smart move, because that money is gonna be worth a LOT more than $3.00 in the future.

So hopefully whoever finds the time capsule will travel back in time and reward me for making them rich.

I wrote a little note and put it in the box just to make sure the person who finds it knows exactly who to thank.

> To whom it may concern:
> The cash is from
> Greg Heffley
> 12 Surrey Street

Me and Rowley found a shoe box and put all of our stuff in it. Then we sealed it up with some masking tape.

I wrote a little note on the outside of the box to make sure it didn't get opened too soon.

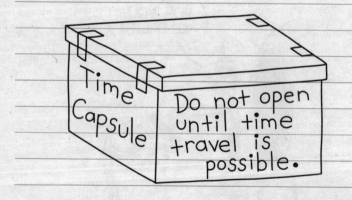

Time Capsule

Do not open until time travel is possible.

After that, we put it in the hole we dug yesterday and buried it as best we could.

I kind of wish Rowley had put some more effort into digging the hole, because our time capsule wasn't really buried all the way. Hopefully nobody will mess with it, because it needs to stay there for at least a few hundred years.

Monday

Well, my week got off to a rough start. When I got out of bed, Mom's bathrobe wasn't where it usually is, hanging on my doorknob.

I asked Mom if she took the robe back, but she said she didn't. So I have a feeling Dad had something to do with it.

A couple of days ago, I figured out a way to combine the bathrobe experience and the heating vent experience, and I don't think Dad really approved of my idea.

AAAAAAAAHHHH!

FWOOSH

I figure he either hid the robe or got rid of it. Now that I think of it, Dad made a run to the Goodwill bin last night after dinner, so that's probably not a good sign.

Anyway, if Dad DID get rid of the robe, it wouldn't be the first time he's thrown out someone's personal property. You know how Manny has been trying to quit using his pacifier?

Yesterday morning Dad got rid of every single one of Manny's binkies.

Well, Manny totally freaked out. The only way Mom could get him to calm down was to dig out his old blanket, this thing he calls "Tingy".

Tingy started off as a blue blanket that Mom knitted for Manny's first birthday, and it was love at first sight.

Manny carried that thing around with him everywhere he went. He wouldn't even let Mom take it away from him so she could WASH it.

It started falling apart, and by the time Manny was two his blanket was basically a couple of pieces of yarn held together by raisins and boogers.

I think that's when Manny started calling his blanket "Tingy".

For the past couple of days, Manny's been dragging Tingy around the house just like he did when he was a baby, and I've been trying to stay out of his way as much as possible.

Wednesday

I'm getting really tired of walking to school every day, so this morning I asked Mom if she would drive me and Rowley. The reason I didn't ask her sooner is because Mom's car is covered in all these embarrassing bumper stickers, and kids at my school are brutal when it comes to that sort of thing.

I've tried scraping the bumper stickers off, but whatever kind of glue they put on those things is meant to last until the end of time.

Today me and Rowley got a ride from Mom, but I told her to let us out BEHIND the school.

Well, I made the dumb mistake of leaving my backpack in the car, so Mom brought it to me in fourth period. And of course she picked TODAY to finally start going to the gym.

It was just my luck, too. Fourth period is the only time I have a class with Holly Hills, and I've been trying to make a good impression on her this year. I figure this incident probably set me back about three weeks.

I'm not the only one who's trying to impress Holly Hills, either. I think just about every boy in my class has a crush on her.

Holly is the fourth-prettiest girl in the class, but the top three all have boyfriends. So a lot of guys like me are doing everything they can to get in good with her.

I've been trying to come up with an angle to separate myself from the rest of the goobers who like Holly. And I think I finally figured it out: humour.

See, the kids in my class are like Neanderthals when it comes to jokes. To give you an idea of what I'm talking about, here's the kind of thing that passes for comedy at my school –

Any time Holly's in the area, I make sure I use my best material.

I've been using Rowley as my comedy partner, and I've actually trained him on a couple of pretty decent jokes.

The only problem is Rowley's starting to get a little greedy about who gets to say what, so I don't know if this partnership is gonna work out long-term.

Friday

Well, I learned my lesson about getting a ride from Mom, so I'm back to walking to school. But when I was heading home with Rowley this afternoon I seriously didn't think I had the energy to make it up the hill to my house. So I asked Rowley if he'd give me a piggyback ride.

Rowley didn't exactly jump at the idea, so I had to remind him that we're best friends and this is the kind of thing best friends do for each other. He finally caved when I offered to carry his backpack for him.

GASP
WHEEZE

I have a feeling this was a one-time thing, though, because Rowley was completely wiped out by the time he dropped me off at my house. You know, if the school is going to take away our bus ride home, the least they could do is install a ski lift on our hill.

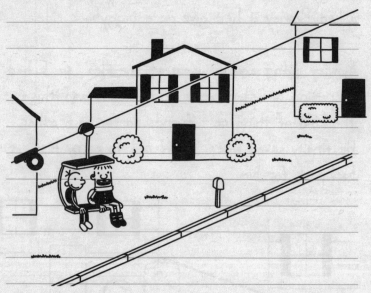

I've e-mailed the principal about five times with my suggestion, but I haven't heard anything back yet.

When I got to my house, I was pretty tired, too. My new thing is that I take a nap every day after school.

In fact, I LIVE for my naps. Sleeping after school is the only way I can really recharge my batteries, and on most days the second I get home, I'm in bed.

AAAAAAAHHH!

I'm actually kind of becoming an expert at sleeping. Once I'm out, I can sleep through just about anything.

The only person I know who's better at sleeping than me is RODRICK, and here's the reason I say that. A couple of weeks ago, Mom had to order Rodrick a new bed because he'd worn his out. So the furniture guys came to take his old mattress and box spring away.

When they came, Rodrick was in the middle of
his after-school nap. So they took his bed
away, and he just slept on the floor, right in
the middle of his empty bed frame.

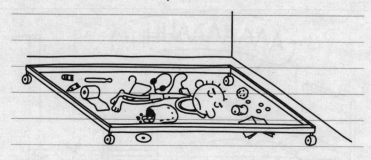

The thing I'm worried about is that Dad is going
to ban our after-school naps. I'm starting to get
the feeling he's sick of waking the two of us up
for dinner every night.

Tuesday
Well, I hate to admit this, but I think my naps
are starting to have an effect on my grades.

48

See, I used to do my homework when I got home from school, and then I watched TV at night. Lately I've been trying to do my homework WHILE I watch TV, and sometimes that doesn't work out too good.

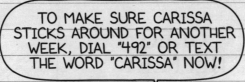

I had this four-page Biology paper due today, but last night I kind of got caught up in this show I was watching. So I had to try to write the whole thing in the computer lab during recess today.

I didn't have a lot of time to do any research, so I played with the margins and the font size to stretch what I had to four pages. But I'm pretty sure Ms Nolan is gonna call me on it.

CHIMPS

A four-page paper by

GREG HEFFLEY

1

This is a chimpanzee, or "chimp" for short.

Chimps are the subject of the paper you're holding in your hand right now.

2

Chimps are supposed to be smart, but I'm not so sure that's true.

3

Well, it looks like I'm out of paper, so I guess this is

THE END.

4

Yesterday I actually got a "zero" on a quiz in Geography. But, in my defence, it was really hard to study for the quiz and watch football at the same time.

To be honest with you, I don't think teachers should be making us memorize all this stuff to begin with, because in the future everyone is going to have a personal robot that tells you whatever you need to know.

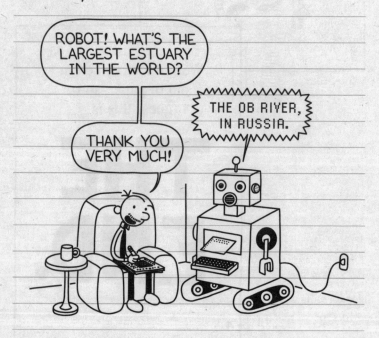

Speaking of teachers, today Mrs Craig was in a really bad mood. That's because the big dictionary that usually sits on her desk was missing.

I'm sure someone just borrowed it and forgot to put it back, but the word Mrs Craig kept using was "stole".

Mrs Craig said that if the dictionary wasn't returned to her desk before the end of the period she was keeping everyone inside for recess.

Then she told us she was going to leave the room, and that if the "culprit" returned the dictionary to her desk there wouldn't be any consequences, and there would be no questions asked.

53

Mrs Craig made Patty Farrell class monitor and left the room. Patty takes her job as class monitor really seriously, and when she's in charge nobody dares to step out of line.

I was just hoping the person who took the dictionary would hurry up and come clean, because I had two cartons of chocolate milk for lunch.

But nobody did come forward. And, sure enough, Mrs Craig stuck to her promise and kept us inside for recess. Then she said she was gonna keep us inside every day until the dictionary was returned.

Friday
Mrs Craig has kept us inside for the past three days, and still no dictionary. Today Patty Farrell was sick, so Mrs Craig put Alex Aruda in charge of the room while she was gone.

Alex is a good student, but people aren't afraid of Alex the way they are of Patty Farrell. As soon as Mrs Craig left the room, it was complete pandemonium.

A couple of guys who were sick of getting stuck inside for recess every day decided to try to figure out who took Mrs Craig's dictionary.

The first person they interrogated was this kid named Corey Lamb. I think Corey was number one on the list of suspects because he's smart and he's always using big words.

Corey fessed up to the crime in no time flat. But it turns out he only said he did it because the pressure made him crack.

SHAKE
SHAKE

SUCK
SUCK

The next kid on the list was Peter Lynn, and before you knew it Peter was confessing, too.

I figured it was just a matter of time before those guys cornered ME. So I knew I had to think up something fast.

I've read enough Sherlock Sammy books to know that sometimes it takes a nerd to get you out of a pinch. And I figured if anyone could crack this case it was Alex Aruda.

So me and a couple of other guys who were worried about getting hassled went over to Alex to see if he could help us out.

We told Alex we needed him to solve the mystery of who took Mrs Craig's dictionary, but he didn't even know what we were TALKING about. I guess Alex had been so wrapped up in his book that he hadn't even noticed what had been going on around him for the past couple of days.

Plus, Alex always stays inside to read during recess, so Mrs Craig's punishment hadn't had a big effect on his life.

Unfortunately, Alex has read his share of Sherlock Sammy books, too, so he said he would help us if we paid him five bucks. Well, that was totally unfair, because Sherlock Sammy only charges a nickel. But me and the other guys agreed it was worth it, and we pooled our money, then forked over the five dollars.

We laid out all the facts of the case to Alex, but we didn't know a whole lot. Then we asked Alex if he could get us pointed in the right direction.

I expected Alex to start taking notes and spout some scientific mumbo jumbo, but all he did was close the book he was reading and show the cover to us. And you're not gonna BELIEVE this, but it was Mrs Craig's dictionary.

Alex said he'd been studying the dictionary to get ready for the state spelling bee next month. Well, THAT would've been nice to know BEFORE we gave him our five bucks. Anyway, there was no time to waste complaining, because Mrs Craig was gonna be back in the room at any second.

Corey Lamb grabbed the book from Alex and put it on Mrs Craig's desk. But she walked in the room right at that moment.

Mrs Craig ended up going back on her whole "no consequences" promise, so Corey Lamb is gonna be spending the next three weeks inside during recess. Looking on the bright side, though, at least he'll have Alex Aruda to keep him company.

FEBRUARY

Tuesday

Yesterday in the cafeteria, when I emptied out my lunch bag, I got TWO FRUITS – and no snacks.

This was a pretty big problem. Mom always packs cookies or sugar wafers or something in my lunch bag, and it's usually the only thing I eat. So I had no energy for the rest of the day.

When I got home, I asked Mom what the deal was with the two-fruits thing. She said she always buys enough treats to last us the whole week, so one of us boys must've taken the snacks out of the bin in the laundry room.

I'm sure Mom thinks I'm the one stealing the snacks, but, believe me, I already learned my lesson about doing THAT.

Last year I took treats out of the bin, but I totally paid the price for it when I opened my lunch bag at school and pulled out Mom's substitute snack.

WOULD ONE OF YOU GENTLEMEN CARE TO TRADE SOMETHING FOR A PACK OF CROUTONS?

Today at lunch it was the same exact thing: two fruits and no snacks.

Like I said, I really depend on the boost I get from that sugar. I almost fell asleep in Mr Watson's class in sixth period, but luckily I snapped awake when my head hit the back of my chair.

When I got home, I told Mom it wasn't fair someone else was eating the treats and I was having to suffer. But she said she wasn't going to go grocery shopping until the end of the week, and that I'd just have to "make do" until then.

Dad wasn't any help, either. When I complained to him, he just made up a penalty for anyone caught stealing snacks, which was "no drums and no video games for a week". So obviously he thinks it's either me or Rodrick.

Like I said, it's not ME, but I figured Dad might be right about Rodrick. When Rodrick went up to the bathroom after dinner, I walked down to his room to see if I could find any wrappers or crumbs.

But while I was poking around in Rodrick's room, I heard him coming downstairs. I had to hide quick, because for some reason Rodrick gets really bent out of shape when he catches me in his room, like he did yesterday.

HEY, LOOK AT ME!

Right before Rodrick got to the bottom of the stairs, I dived into his desk cabinet and shut the door. Rodrick walked in the room, then flopped on his bed and called his friend Ward.

Rodrick and Ward talked FOREVER, and I was starting to think I might have to spend the night in that desk.

Rodrick and Ward got into a pretty heated debate about whether or not a person could throw up while standing on their head, and I started to feel like I was gonna throw up myself. Luckily, right around then, the phone's battery died. When Rodrick went upstairs to get the spare phone, I made a run for it.

This snack thing wouldn't even be an issue if I had money. If I did, I could just buy something from the vending machine at school every day.

At the moment, though, I'm kind of broke. That's because I wasted all my money on some junk I can't even USE.

About a month ago, I saw these ads in the back of one of my comic books, and I sent away for a couple of things that were supposed to TOTALLY change my life.

I started receiving my stuff in the mail about two weeks ago.

The Cash Machine turned out to be some stupid magic trick where you have to insert your OWN money in this secret slot for it to work. And that wasn't good, because I was really counting on that thing to get me out of having to find a job when I grow up.

The X-Ray Goggles just made you see blurry and cross-eyed, so that was a bust, too.

The Throw Your Voice thing didn't work at ALL, even though I followed the instructions in the book.

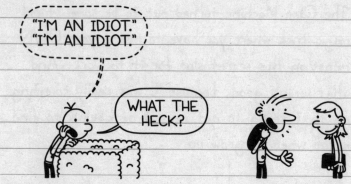

But the item I had the highest hopes for was the Personal Hovercraft. I figured getting home after school would be a breeze once my hovercraft finally showed up in the mail.

Well, I got the package today, but there wasn't a hovercraft inside. There was just a blueprint for how to BUILD a hovercraft, and I got stuck on Step One.

Step One:

Acquire an industrial twin-turbine engine.

I just can't believe the people who write those ads can get away with lying to kids like that. I thought about hiring a lawyer to sue those guys, but lawyers cost money and, like I said before, the Cash Machine was a piece of garbage.

Thursday
Today, when I got home from school, Mom was waiting for me, and she didn't look too happy. It turns out the school sent home mid-term report cards, and she got the mail before I could intercept it.

Mom showed me the report card, and it wasn't pretty. Then she said we were gonna wait for DAD to get home to see what HE thought.

Man, waiting for Dad to get home when you're in trouble is the WORST. I used to just hide in the closet, but recently I figured out a better way to handle it. Now, whenever I get in trouble, I ask Gramma to come over for dinner, because Dad's not gonna act mad at me if Gramma's around.

WHY, AREN'T YOU A DEAR?

At dinner, I made sure I sat in the seat right next to Gramma.

Luckily, Mom didn't mention my report card during dinner. And when Gramma said she needed to leave to go to Bingo, I tagged right along with her.

CATCH YOU GUYS LATER!

Escaping Dad wasn't the ONLY reason I went to Bingo with Gramma. I also went because I needed a surefire way to make some money.

I figured spending a few hours with Gramma and her Bingo friends was a pretty fair price to pay for a week's worth of snacks from the vending machine in the school cafeteria.

Gramma and her friends are EXPERTS at Bingo, and they're real serious about it, too. They have all sorts of gear like lucky blotters and "Bingo Trolls" and stuff like that to help them win.

One of Gramma's friends is so good that she memorizes all her cards, and she doesn't even NEED to use a blotter to mark them off.

For some reason, tonight Gramma and her friends weren't winning like they usually do. But then on the "Cover All" game, I got every square. I yelled out "BINGO" real loud, and the clerk came over to check my card.

It turns out I messed up and covered a couple of squares that I shouldn't have. The clerk announced that my win was no good, and everyone else in the room was pretty happy that they could keep playing.

Gramma told me not to call so much attention to myself if I called out "Bingo" again, because the regulars don't like it when a newcomer wins.

I thought Gramma was pulling my leg, but, sure enough, the regulars sent one of their ladies over to intimidate me. And I have to admit she did her job really well.

Friday

Well, today wasn't exactly my best day ever. For starters, I flunked my Science test. So it probably would've been a good idea to have studied last night instead of spending four hours at Bingo.

I fell asleep in sixth period today, and this time I was out COLD - Mr Watson had to shake me to get me to wake up. As a punishment, I had to sit in the front of the room.

That was just fine with me, because at least up there I could sleep in peace.

I just wish someone had woken me up when sixth period ended, because I didn't wake up until the NEXT period started.

The class I woke up in was taught by Mrs Lowry. Mrs Lowry gave me detention, and on Monday I'm gonna have to stay after school to serve it.

Tonight I was totally jittery from my sugar withdrawal, but I didn't have any money to go buy a soda or candy from the convenience store. So I did something I'm not real proud of.

I went to Rowley's and dug up the time capsule we buried in his front yard. But I only did it because I was desperate.

I took the time capsule back to my house, opened it up and got out my three bucks. Then I went down to the convenience store and bought myself a big soda, a pack of gummy bears and a candy bar.

I guess I feel a little bad that the time capsule me and Rowley put together didn't stay buried for a few hundred years. On the other hand, it's kind of neat that one of US got to open it, because we had actually put some really good stuff in there.

Monday

I didn't really know what to expect from detention, but when I walked into the room, the first thought I had was: I don't belong in here with these future criminals.

I took the only empty seat, which was right in front of this kid named Leon Ricket.

Leon is not the brightest kid in our school. He was in detention because of what he did when a wasp landed on the window in homeroom.

I found out that all you do in detention is sit there and wait for it to be over. You're not allowed to read or do your homework or ANYTHING, which is a pretty dumb rule, considering that most of the kids in there could really use the extra study time.

Mr Ray was the moderator, and he more or less kept an eye on us. But every time Mr Ray looked away, Leon would flick my ear or give me a Wet Willie or something like that. Eventually Leon got careless, and Mr Ray caught Leon with his finger in my ear.

Mr Ray said if he caught Leon touching me again he was gonna be in BIG trouble.

I knew Leon was just gonna go back to bugging me, so I decided to put a stop to it. As soon as Mr Ray's back was turned, I slapped my hands together to make it seem like Leon had hit me.

Mr Ray turned round and told Leon he was gonna have to stay another half hour, and that he had detention again TOMORROW.

On the way home, I was wondering if I'd made the smartest move back there at the school. I'm not exactly the fastest runner, and a half hour isn't that big of a head start.

Tuesday
Tonight I realized ALL of my current problems can be traced back to when someone in my family started stealing the lunch snacks. So I decided to catch the thief once and for all.

I knew Mom had gone grocery shopping over the weekend, so there was a fresh supply of snacks in the laundry room. That meant the snack thief was pretty much guaranteed to strike.

After dinner I went in the laundry room and turned off the light. Then I climbed in an empty basket and waited.

About a half hour later, someone came in the room and turned on the light, so I hid under a towel. But it turns out it was just Mom.

I stayed perfectly still while she got clothes out of the dryer. Mom didn't notice me in there, and she dumped the clothes from the dryer right into the basket where I was hiding.

DUMP

Then she walked out of the room, and I waited some more. I was seriously ready to wait there all night if that's what it took.

But the clothes from the dryer were really warm, and I started feeling a little drowsy. And before I knew it I was asleep.

ZZZZZ

I don't know how many hours I slept, but what I DO know is that I woke up to the sound of crinkling cellophane.

When I heard the sound of chewing, I turned on my flashlight and caught the thief red-handed.

It was Dad! Man, I should have known it was him from the start. When it comes to junk food, he's a total ADDICT.

I started to give Dad a piece of my mind, but he cut me off. He wasn't interested in talking about why he was stealing our lunch snacks. What he WAS interested in talking about was what the heck I was doing buried in a pile of Mom's underwear in the middle of the night.

Right at that moment, we heard Mom coming down the stairs.

I think me and Dad realized how bad the situation looked for both of us, so we each just grabbed as many oatmeal creams as we could carry and made a run for it.

Wednesday
I was still really steamed at Dad for stealing our lunch treats, and I was planning on confronting him tonight. But Dad was in bed by 6:00, so I didn't get my chance.

Dad went to bed so early because he was depressed about something that had happened when he got home from work. When Dad was getting the mail, our neighbours from up the street, the Snellas, walked down the hill with their new baby.

HEY THERE, FRANK!

The baby's name is Seth, and I think he's about two months old.

Every time the Snellas have a baby, six months later they throw a big "half-birthday" party and invite all the neighbours.

The highlight of each Snella half-birthday party is when the adults line up and try to make the baby laugh. The grown-ups do all these wacky things and make COMPLETE fools of themselves.

GOO GOO GOO GOO GOO!

I've been to every single Snella half-birthday party so far, and no baby has laughed once.

Everyone knows the REAL reason the Snellas have these half-birthday parties is because their big dream is to win the $10,000 Grand Prize on "America's Funniest Families". That's this TV show where they play home movies of people getting hit in the groin with golf balls and stuff like that.

The Snellas are just hoping something really funny will happen at one of their parties so they can catch it on videotape. They've actually got some pretty good stuff over the years. During Sam Snella's half-birthday party, Mr Bittner split his trousers doing jumping jacks. And, during Scott Snella's party, Mr Odom was walking backwards, and he fell in the baby pool.

WWAAUUGH!

WHIRR

The Snellas turned in those videos, but they didn't win anything. So I guess they're just gonna keep having babies until they do.

Dad HATES performing in front of people, so he'll do everything he can to avoid having to act like a fool in front of the whole neighbourhood. And, so far, Dad has weaselled his way out of every single Snella half-birthday party.

At dinner, Mom told Dad he HAS to go to Seth Snella's half-birthday party in June. And I'm pretty sure Dad knows that this time his number is finally up.

Thursday
Everybody at school has been talking about the big Valentine's Dance that's coming up next week.

This is the first year at my school that they've actually had a dance, so everyone's all excited. Some of the guys in my class were even asking girls if they would be their dates to the dance.

Me and Rowley are both bachelors at the moment, but that's not gonna stop us from arriving in style.

I figured if me and Rowley scraped together some money in the next few days, we could rent a limo for the night. But, when I called the limo company, the guy who answered the phone called me "ma'am". So that pretty much blew any chance he had of getting MY business.

Since the dance is next week, I realized I was gonna need something to wear.

I'm kind of in a pinch because I've already worn most of the clothes I got for Christmas, and I'm almost out of clean stuff to wear. I went through my dirty clothes to see if there was anything I could wear a SECOND time.

I separated my laundry into two piles: one that I could wear again, and one that would get me sent down to Nurse Powell's office for a lecture on hygiene.

I found a shirt in pile number one that wasn't so bad, except it had a jam stain on the left-hand side. So at the dance I'll just need to remember to keep Holly Hills to the right of me at all times.

Valentine's Day

I was up late last night making Valentine's cards for everyone in my class. I'm pretty sure my middle school is the only one in the state that still makes all the kids give cards to one another.

Last year I was actually looking forward to the card swap. The night before Valentine's Day, I spent a lot of time making an awesome card for this girl named Natasha who I kind of liked.

♡ Beloved Natasha — For you, a fire blazes in my heart So strong that the embers alone could bring a thousand hot tubs to a boil So intense that it causes snowmen everywhere to despair	Let the bonfire of my love wrap you in its warmth Only your kiss could quench the flames that so consume me To you I pledge my love, my desire, my life 🌹 Greg

I showed Mom my card to check for spelling errors, but she said what I wrote wasn't "age appropriate". She told me maybe I should just get Natasha a little box of candy or something, but I wasn't about to take romantic advice from my mother.

At school everyone went around the room and put their Valentine's cards in one another's boxes, but I delivered my card to Natasha personally.

I let her read it, and then I waited to see what she made for ME.

Natasha dug around in her box and pulled out this cheap store-bought card that was supposed to be for her friend Chantelle, who was out sick that day.

Then Natasha scribbled out her friend's name
and put MY name on it instead.

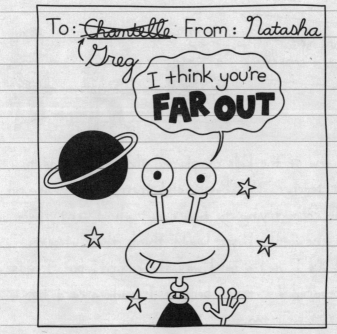

To: ~~Chantelle~~ Greg From: Natasha

I think you're FAR OUT

Anyway, you can probably see why I wasn't too
enthusiastic about the card exchange THIS year.

Last night I came up with a great idea. I
knew I had to make a card for everyone in the
class, but, instead of being all mushy and saying
things I didn't really mean, I told everyone
EXACTLY what I thought of them.

The trick was, I didn't actually SIGN any of my cards.

A few of the kids complained about the cards to our teacher, Mrs Riser, and then she went around the room trying to figure out who'd sent them. I knew Mrs Riser would think that whoever DIDN'T get a card was the culprit, but I was prepared for that, because I made a card for MYSELF, too.

After the card exchange came the Valentine's Dance. The dance was originally supposed to be at NIGHT, but I guess they couldn't get enough parents to volunteer to be chaperones. So they put the dance smack in the middle of the school day instead.

The teachers started rounding everyone up and sending them down to the auditorium at around 1:00. Anyone who didn't want to cough up the two bucks for admission had to go down to Mr Ray's room for study hall.

But it was pretty obvious to most of us that "study hall" was basically the same thing as detention.

The rest of us filed into the gym and sat in the bleachers. I don't know why, but all the boys sat on one side of the gym, and all the girls sat on the other. Once everyone was inside the gym, the teachers started the music. But whoever picked out the songs is SERIOUSLY out of touch with what kids are listening to these days.

YOU DO THE HOKEY POKEY AND YOU TURN YOURSELF AROUND...

For the first fifteen minutes or so, no one moved a muscle. Then Mr Phillips, the guidance counsellor, and Nurse Powell walked to the middle of the gym and started dancing.

I guess Mr Phillips and Nurse Powell thought if THEY started dancing all the kids would come down onto the floor and join them. All they REALLY did was GUARANTEE that everyone stayed in their seat.

Finally, Mrs Mancy, the principal, grabbed a microphone and made an announcement. She said that everyone in the bleachers was REQUIRED to come down onto the floor and dance, and it would count for 20% of our Phys Ed grades.

At that point me and a couple of other boys tried to sneak out to go down to Mr Ray's room, but we got caught by some teachers who were blocking the exits.

Mrs Mancy wasn't kidding about the gym-grade thing, either. She was walking around with Mr Underwood, the Phys Ed teacher, and he was carrying his gradebook with him.

I'm already close to flunking Phys Ed, so I knew it was time to get serious. But I didn't want to look like a fool in front of the kids in my class, either. So I just came up with the simplest move I could do that would technically qualify as "dancing".

Unfortunately, a bunch of guys who were worried about THEIR Phys Ed grades saw what I was doing, and they came over to where I was. And the next thing I knew I was surrounded by a bunch of bozos who were stealing my moves.

STEP   STEP   STEP   STEP

I wanted to get as far away from those guys as I could, so I looked around the gym for a place where I could go to dance in peace.

That's when I spotted Holly Hills across the room, and I remembered why I even bothered coming to the dance in the first place.

Holly was dancing with her friends in the middle of the gym, and I started doing my step-dance thing, moving slowly towards them.

All the girls were lumped together in one big pack, and they were dancing like professionals, probably because they spend all their free time watching MTV.

Holly was right in the middle of the group. I kind of danced around the outside of the circle for a while, trying to find an opening, but I couldn't.

Finally, Holly stopped dancing and went to get a drink, and I knew it was my big chance.

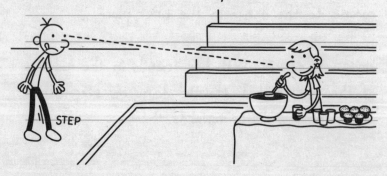

STEP

But, just when I was about to go up to Holly and say something witty, Fregley came flying in out of NOWHERE.

BOOGIE BOOGIE BOOGIE!

Fregley had pink frosting covering his face, so he was probably all hopped-up on sugar from the cupcakes they were serving at the refreshments table. All I know for sure is that he TOTALLY ruined what should have been a great moment between me and Holly.

A few minutes later, the dance was over, and I missed my chance to make a good impression on her. I walked home alone after school, because I just needed a little time by myself.

After dinner Mom told me there was a Valentine's card out in the mailbox with my name on it. When I asked her who it was from, she just said, "Someone special." I ran out to the mailbox and got the card, and I have to admit I was pretty excited. I was hoping it was from Holly, but there are at least four or five other girls at my school who I wouldn't mind getting a card from, either.

The card was in a big pink envelope with my name written in cursive. I ripped it open, and here's what I found: a sheet of construction paper with a piece of candy taped to it, and it was from ROWLEY.

Sometimes I just don't know about that boy.

MARCH

<u>Saturday</u>

The other day Dad found Manny's blanket, Tingy, on the couch. I don't think Dad knew what it was, so he threw it away.

Ever since then Manny's been turning the house upside down looking for his blanket, and finally Dad had to tell him that he accidentally threw it out. Well, Manny got his revenge yesterday by using Dad's Civil War battlefield as a playset.

Manny's been taking his anger out on everyone else, too. Today I was sitting on the couch just minding my own business, and Manny walked up to me and said –

I didn't know if "Ploopy" was some kind of little-kid bad word or what, but I didn't like the sound of it. So I went to find Mom and ask her if SHE knew what it meant.

Unfortunately, Mom was on the phone, and when she's gabbing with one of her friends it takes forever to get her attention.

I finally got Mom to stop talking for a second, but she was mad that I interrupted her. I told her Manny called me "Ploopy", and she said –

WHAT IS A PLOOPY?

That kind of threw me for a second, because it's the exact question I was trying to ask HER. I didn't have an answer, so Mom just went back to her conversation.

After that, Manny knew he had a green light to call me Ploopy whenever he wanted, and that's what he's been doing all day.

WIPE MY HEINIE, PLOOPY!

I guess I should've known that telling on Manny wasn't gonna get me anywhere. When me and Rodrick were little, we used to tell on each other so much that it made Mom crazy. So she brought out this thing called the Tattle Turtle to solve the problem.

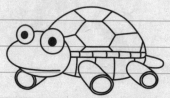

Mom came up with the Tattle Turtle idea when she taught pre-school. The idea behind the Tattle Turtle was that if me and Rodrick had a problem with each other we had to tell the Tattle Turtle instead of Mom. Well, the Tattle Turtle worked out GREAT for Rodrick, but not so much for me.

TATTLE TURTLE, RODRICK STOLE ALL THE MONEY FROM MY PIGGY BANK!

<u>Easter</u>

On the car ride to church today, I felt like I was sitting on something sticky. And when I got out and turned round to look at the back of my trousers there was chocolate ALL OVER them.

Manny had brought his Easter bunny with him in the car, and I must've been sitting on an ear or something.

Mom was trying to get the family inside so we could get good seats, but I told her there was no WAY I was going in there looking like that.

I knew Holly Hills and her family were probably already there, and I really didn't need her wondering if I'd pooped in my pants.

Mom said skipping church on Easter wasn't an option, and we argued back and forth. Then Rodrick chimed in with HIS solution.

Rodrick knows that church on Easter is always at least two hours long, so he was just looking for an excuse to get out of it. But, right at that moment, Dad's boss and his family pulled up alongside us in the parking lot.

Mom made Rodrick put his trousers back on, and then she gave me her sweater to tie around my waist.

I don't know which was worse: wearing dress pants with chocolate all over them or wearing Mom's pink Easter sweater like a kilt.

Church was pretty full. The only seats that were empty were right up front where Uncle Joe and his family were sitting, so we sat next to them.

I looked around, and I spotted Holly Hills and her family three rows back. I was pretty sure she couldn't see what I was wearing from the waist down, so that was a relief.

As soon as the music started up, Uncle Joe reached out to hold hands with me and his wife, and he started singing.

I tried to break free a couple of times, but Uncle Joe had an iron grip. The song was only like a minute long, but to me it felt like half an hour.

After the song was over, I turned to the people behind us, pointed at Uncle Joe and made the "cuckoo" sign so everyone knew I wasn't on board with this holding-hands thing.

TWIRL

Somewhere in the middle of church, they passed a basket around so people could give money to help the needy.

I didn't have any money of my own, so I whispered to Mom to see if she would give me a dollar. Then, when the basket came to me, I made a big deal of putting the dollar in the basket to make sure Holly could see how generous I was.

But when I put the money in the basket, I realized Mom had given me a TWENTY, not a single. I tried to grab the basket to make change, but it was too late.

All I can say is, I better get some points in Heaven for THAT donation.

I've heard that when you do good deeds you're supposed to be all private about it, but that doesn't really make a whole lot of sense to ME.

If I start hiding my good deeds, I'm sure I'll just regret it later on.

BUT WHAT ABOUT THAT SQUIRREL I HELPED WITH THE BROKEN LEG?

SORRY... I MUST'VE MISSED THAT.

Like I said before, the Easter service is SUPER long. One of the songs was going on for about five minutes, and I started looking for ways to entertain myself.

The way that Rodrick keeps himself busy when he's bored is by picking at this scab on the back of his hand that he never lets heal, but I'm not really interested in going that route.

Manny has it MADE in church. Mom and Dad let him bring all sorts of stuff with us to keep him entertained. Believe me, Mom and Dad never let me bring anything to church when I was his age.

Mom and Dad ALWAYS baby Manny, though, and I'll give you an example of what I'm talking about. Last week Manny was at pre-school, and when he opened up his lunchbox his sandwich was cut in HALF, not in QUARTERS, the way he likes it.

Manny threw a huge temper tantrum, and the teachers had to call Mom. So she left work and drove all the way down to Manny's school to make the extra slice.

Anyway, I was thinking about this at church, and all of a sudden I got an idea in my head. I leaned over to Manny and whispered –

Well, Manny completely LOST it.

He started BAWLING, and everyone in the church turned their heads our way. Even the minister stopped talking to see what was going on.

Mom couldn't calm Manny down, so we had to leave. Instead of walking out the side door, though, we walked right down the centre aisle.

I tried to look as cool as possible when we walked past the Hills family, but it was pretty tough, considering the circumstances.

The only person more embarrassed than me was Dad. Dad tried to cover his face with the church bulletin, but his boss spotted him and gave Dad the "thumbs up" on the way out.

<u>Wednesday</u>

Things have kind of been tense around the house since the mess the other day. First of all, Mom was really mad at me for calling Manny "Ploopy", so I had to remind her that she didn't have any problem when MANNY said it. So Mom banned the word for everyone, and she said that if anyone was caught saying it they'd be grounded for a week. But of course it didn't take long for Rodrick to find a loophole.

114

This isn't the FIRST time Mom has banned us from saying certain words in the house. A while back, Mom made a "no swearing" rule, because Manny was picking up new words left and right.

Every time someone said a bad word in front of Manny, they had to put a dollar in his "Swear Jar". So Manny was getting rich off me and Rodrick.

And then Mom upped the ante by banning words like "stupid" and "jerk" and stuff like that.

To keep from going bankrupt, me and Rodrick came up with a bunch of code words that meant the same thing as the banned words, and we've been using them ever since.

Every once in a while, I forget to switch back when I get to school, and I end up looking dumb. Just today, David Nester spat out a piece of gum and it landed in my hair. I really let loose with everything I had, but I don't think I upset David too much.

The other thing that's changed since Easter is that Dad has been on me and Rodrick's case. I guess he's tired of us looking bad in front of his boss, Mr Warren.

Dad made Rodrick enroll in an SAT class, and he made ME sign up for Rec League soccer.

Soccer tryouts were tonight. The coaches lined up all the kids for a "skills test", where you had to dribble the ball between some cones and stuff like that.

I tried my best, but I got ranked "Pre-Alpha Minus", which I'm sure is just adult code words for "You Stink".

After the skills test, they put us on different teams. I was hoping I'd get one of those fun coaches who doesn't take sports too seriously, like Mr Proctor or Mr Gibb, but I got the worst one out of the whole bunch, Mr Litch.

Mr Litch is one of these drill-sergeant types who likes to yell a lot. Mr Litch used to be Rodrick's coach, and he's pretty much the reason Rodrick doesn't do sports any more.

Anyway, our first real practice is tomorrow. Hopefully, I'll just get cut so I can get back to playing video games. Twisted Wizard 2 is supposed to come out soon, and I heard it's AWESOME.

Thursday
I got put on a team with a bunch of kids I
didn't really know. The first thing Mr Litch did
was hand out uniforms, and then he told us to
come up with a team name.

I suggested that we call our team the "Twisted
Wizards", and get the Game Hut to sponsor us.

Nobody liked my idea, though. One kid said we
should call the team the "Red Sox", which I
thought was a terrible idea. Number one, the Red
Sox are a BASEBALL team and, number two, our
soccer uniforms are BLUE.

But of course everyone else LOVED the idea, and
that's the name that won out. Then the assistant
coach, Mr Boone, said he was worried that if we
called our team the Red Sox we might get sued.

I'm pretty sure those guys have better things to do than to go around suing middle-school soccer teams, but, like I said before, nobody wanted to listen to MY opinions.

So the team voted to change the name to "Red SOCKS", and that was final.

After that we started practice. Mr Litch and Mr Boone made us run laps and do leg-lifts and a bunch of other stuff that had nothing to do with soccer. In between wind sprints, I hung out by the water cooler with the other two Pre-Alpha Minus guys. And every time we were slow getting back to the field Mr Litch would yell –

GET YOUR BUTTS OVER HERE!

Me and the other guys thought it would be pretty funny if the next time Mr Litch said that we all ran at him with our butts sticking out.

So the next time Mr Litch yelled for us to get our butts over there, I ran with my rear end pointed at him. But the other guys TOTALLY hung me out to dry.

Mr Litch did not appreciate my sense of humour, and he made me run three extra laps.

When Dad picked me up at the end of practice, I told him that maybe this soccer thing wasn't such a good idea, and that he should probably just let me quit.

That made Dad pretty mad, so he said -

NO SON OF MINE IS A QUITTER!

Which isn't really true at all. I'm a HUGE quitter, and so is Rodrick. And I think Manny is on his third or fourth pre-school by now.

Anyway, I got the feeling that if I'm gonna get out of soccer I'm gonna have to think of another angle.

Friday
Ever since I started playing soccer, I've been going through my clothes twice as quick as I did before. I've been totally out of clean stuff to wear for a while now, so I've been pulling all of my clothes out of my dirty laundry piles. But I found out today that recycling clothes from the dirty laundry pile can be risky.

I was walking by some girls in the hallway today, and a pair of dirty underwear fell out of one of my trouser legs. I just kept walking and hoped that the girls might think the underwear wasn't actually mine.

But I paid the price for THAT decision later on in the day.

I think I'd better hurry up and learn how to do my laundry, because I'm really running out of options. Tomorrow I'm gonna have to wear a T-shirt I got from my Uncle Gary's first wedding, and I'm really not looking forward to it.

I was kind of down in the dumps on the walk home from school today, but then something happened to change that. Rowley told me one of his friends from karate was having a sleepover this weekend, and he asked me if I wanted to come along.

I was about to say "no way", but then Rowley
said something that got my attention. The kid
who's having the party lives on Pleasant Street,
which is in the same neighbourhood that Holly Hills
lives in.

At lunch today I overheard a couple of girls saying
that HOLLY is having a sleepover Saturday night,
so this could really be the opportunity of a
LIFETIME for me.

Tonight at soccer practice, Mr Litch told everyone the position they'd be playing in the first game on Sunday.

Mr Litch told me I'd be the "Fetcher", and that sounded pretty cool to me. So, when I got home, I bragged to Rodrick about it.

I thought Rodrick would be impressed, but he just laughed. He told me that Fetcher wasn't actually a real position on the field — it's just a kid who chases the ball when it goes out of bounds. Then he showed me a rulebook with all the soccer positions and, sure enough, Fetcher wasn't in it.

Rodrick is always pulling my leg, so I guess I'll just have to wait until this weekend to see if he's telling the truth this time.

Sunday
Remind me to never go to a sleepover with Rowley again.

Yesterday afternoon Mom dropped me and Rowley off at his friend's house. The first hint that I was in for a long night was when we walked into the house and there wasn't a kid there who was older than six.

My SECOND hint was that everyone was wearing their karate gear.

The whole reason I even WENT to this sleepover was so we could all sneak out and crash Holly's slumber party. But Rowley's friends were more interested in "Sesame Street" than they were in girls.

All those guys wanted to do was play a bunch of dopey party games, like Blind Man's Bluff and that kind of thing. I could've been playing Spin the Bottle with Holly Hills, but instead I spent my night trying not to get groped by a bunch of first-graders.

Rowley's friends played some other games, too, like Freeze Tag and Twister.

I excused myself to go upstairs when someone suggested we could play Who Licked Me?

I tried calling Mom to come pick me up, but she was out with Dad. So I knew I was stuck at this kid's house for the night.

At about 9:30 I decided to just go to sleep and get the night over with. But those guys came into the bedroom and got into a massive pillow fight. And, let me tell you, it's not easy falling asleep when a sweaty little kid falls on you every five seconds.

KICK

Eventually the kid's mom came upstairs and told everyone it was time to go to sleep.

Even after the lights went out, Rowley and his friends stayed up, talking and giggling. They must have thought I fell asleep, because at one point a bunch of them snuck up on me to try and pull the hand-in-a-bowl-of-warm-water trick.

Well, that was enough for ME. I went downstairs to sleep in the basement, even though it was pitch-black down there and I couldn't find the light. I'd left my sleeping bag upstairs, and that was a mistake, because it was FREEZING in the basement.

I did NOT want to go back upstairs and get my stuff, though. I just curled up in a ball and tried to conserve as much body heat as possible to make it through to the morning.

I think it was probably the longest night of my life.

When the sun came up this morning, I found out the reason it was so cold in the basement. I was sleeping right by the sliding glass door, and some fool had gone and left it open overnight.

That really stunk, because if I knew there was a way to escape last night, I DEFINITELY would've taken it.

When I got home this morning, I went back to bed until Dad woke me up and told me it was time to go to the soccer game.

It turns out Rodrick was right about the Fetcher thing. I spent the whole game pulling balls out of the brambles and, let me tell you, it wasn't a whole lot of fun.

Our team won the game, and afterwards we were supposed to go out to celebrate. Dad couldn't stick around, so he asked Mr Litch if he would drive me home afterwards.

Well, I really wish Dad had asked ME what I thought about that idea first, because I would've just gone home with him.

I was starving from all that digging around in the bushes, though, so I figured I'd just go with the team.

We went to a fast-food place, and I ordered twenty chicken nuggets. I went to use the bathroom, and when I came back to the table all my food was gone. But then Erick Bickford dumped my nuggets out of his big sweaty hands.

If you ever wanted to know why I don't like team sports, there it is in a nutshell.

After lunch was over, me, Kenny Keith and Erick got into Mr Litch's car. Kenny sat in the back with Erick, and I sat up front in the passenger seat.

We had to wait a long time because Mr Litch was sitting on the hood of his car, blabbing away with Mr Boone. After we'd been sitting there for a while, Kenny leaned forward from the back seat and pressed the horn for about three seconds.

Then Kenny jumped back in his seat so when Mr Litch turned round it looked like I was the one who honked the horn.

Mr Litch gave me a dirty look, and then turned back round and talked to his assistant for another half hour.

On the way home, Mr Litch stopped to do about five errands. He wasn't in any hurry to get them done, either.

And get this: Kenny and Erick were mad at ME for making them get home so late. So that should give you a feeling for the type of intelligence I'm dealing with here.

Mr Litch dropped me off last. On the way up the hill, I saw the Snellas out in their front yard, and it looked like they were trying to get some clips to send in to "America's Funniest Families."

I guess they don't feel like waiting around a few months until Seth's half-birthday party.

APRIL

Thursday

Today was April 1st, and here's how my day
started –

Every other day of the year, you couldn't
DRAG Rodrick out of bed before 8:00 a.m. But
on April 1st Rodrick always wakes up early so he
can get his tricks in.

Someone seriously needs to explain the concept of a
practical joke to Rodrick, because all his "jokes"
involve me getting injured.

Last year Rodrick bet me fifty cents I couldn't
tie my shoes while I was standing up, and I
TOTALLY fell for it.

I went inside and told Dad that Rodrick shot me in the butt with a paintball gun. Dad didn't feel like getting in the middle of a fight, so he just told Rodrick to pay me my fifty cents for winning the bet.

Rodrick took two quarters out of his pocket and threw them on the ground. But obviously I hadn't learned my lesson, because I bent over to pick them up.

At least I put some thinking into MY practical jokes. Last year I pulled a pretty good trick on Rowley. We were in the bathroom at a movie theatre, and I convinced him that some random guy standing at the urinal was a professional athlete.

So Rowley asked the guy for his autograph.

And today me and a couple of other guys pulled a good one on Chirag Gupta.

We decided it would be pretty funny if we made him think he was losing his hearing, so we all made sure we talked real quiet every time he came around.

Chirag figured out what was going on pretty quick, and he went straight to the teacher to shut it down before the joke could get out of hand. I guess he didn't want a repeat of the Invisible Chirag joke from last year.

Friday
We had our second soccer game tonight. Some adult volunteered to fetch the balls, so I got to sit on the bench for the whole game.

It was REALLY cold out, and I asked Dad if I could go get my coat out of the car, but he said no.

Dad said I needed to be prepared in case the coach decided to put me in the game, so I had to just tough it out.

I wanted to tell Dad that the only time I'd be stepping foot on the field would be when Mr Litch made me pick up all the other kids' orange peels at halftime. But I just kept quiet and concentrated on not letting my shin guards freeze to my legs.

Every time Mr Litch called a huddle, Dad made me get off the bench and go join the rest of the team. Have you seen a game on TV and wondered what the benchwarmers were thinking when they stand in the huddle while the coach goes over the game plan?

Well, now I can tell you firsthand.

Once the sun went down, it got REALLY
cold. In fact, it got so cold Mackey Creavey
and Manuel Gonzales went and got SLEEPING
BAGS out of the Creaveys' car.

And Dad STILL wouldn't even let me go get
my coat.

During a timeout, we all joined the huddle. And when the coach got an eyeful of Mackey and Manuel he told them they were excused and to go to the Creaveys' car for the rest of the game.

HOP
HOP

HOP
HOP

So Mackey and Manuel got to sit in a heated SUV, while I had to sit on a cold metal bench in my shorts. And I know for a FACT that the Creaveys have a TV in their car, so I'm sure those guys were totally living it up in there.

<u>Monday</u>

I have DEFINITELY got to start keeping on top of my laundry. I've been out of clean underwear for about three days, so I've been wearing my bathing suit as a substitute.

Today we had Phys Ed, and when we changed into our gym clothes, I totally forgot I was wearing my Speedo underneath.

It could have been a lot WORSE, though. I have a pair of Wonder Woman Underoos that I've never taken out of their wrapper, and this morning I was pretty tempted to wear them just because they were clean.

Believe me, I didn't ASK for the Wonder Woman Underoos, either. This past summer a few of my relatives asked Mom what I wanted for my birthday, and she told them I was really into comics and super heroes.

So the Underoos were a gift from Uncle Charlie.

We had another soccer game after school, but it's been getting a lot warmer lately, and I wasn't worried about the cold.

At school, me, Mackey and Manuel agreed we'd all bring some video games tonight, and for the first time we actually ENJOYED ourselves at soccer.

It didn't last long, though. Twenty minutes into the game, Mr Litch called all three of us off the bench and told us to get on the field.

CREAVEY!
HEFFLEY!
GONZALES!

Apparently, some parent complained that their kid wasn't getting any playing time, so the Rec League made a rule that now EVERY kid has to get in the game.

Well, none of us had been paying any attention to the game, so when we got on the field, we didn't know what to do or where to stand.

A couple of kids on our team told us the other team had a "free kick", and that we were supposed to stand shoulder to shoulder to make a shield to block it.

I thought the guys on my team were joking, but it turns out they weren't. Me, Manuel and Mackey had to line up in front of our goal. Then the referee blew the whistle, and a kid from the other team ran at the ball and kicked it right at us.

TWEET!

Well, we didn't do a really good job of protecting the goal, and the other team scored.

Mr Litch pulled the three of us out of the game the second he got the chance, and he yelled at us for not standing still and blocking the ball.

But I'll tell you what: if I have to choose between getting yelled at or getting hit in the face with a soccer ball, it's no contest.

Thursday

After the game last week, I asked Mr Litch if I could be the back-up goalie for the team, and he said I could.

It was a genius move on my part, for a couple of reasons. First of all, goalies don't have to run laps and all that stuff during practice. They just do individual goalie drills with the assistant coach.

Second, goalies wear different uniforms from the rest of the team, and that means Mr Litch can't put me in the game when it's time to block free kicks.

CREAVEY!
GONZALES!

Our regular goalie, Tucker Fox, is the star of the team, so I knew there was no way I was gonna see any playing time, anyway. These last few games have actually been kind of FUN. But tonight something bad happened. Tucker hurt his hand diving after a ball, and he had to come out. So that meant the coach had to put ME in.

Well, Dad was REALLY excited I was finally getting some real playing time, and he came down to my end of the field to coach me from the sideline. It's not like I really needed it, though. Our team kept the ball on the other side of the field for the whole rest of the game, and I didn't even touch it ONCE.

MAKE SURE YOU BEND YOUR KNEES, GREG!

I think I know what Dad was up to, though.

When I used to play T-Ball, I had a really hard time concentrating on the game. Tonight Dad just wanted to make sure I didn't get distracted the way I used to get when I played right field.

I have to admit, it was probably a good thing that Dad stayed on my case tonight.

There were about a MILLION dandelions down at my end of the field, and in the second half I was starting to get a little twitchy.

Monday

Well, yesterday we had another soccer game, and luckily Dad wasn't there to see it. We lost our first game of the season, 1-0. Somehow the other team got the ball past me in the last few seconds, and they won. So that ruined our perfect record.

Afterwards, everyone on my team was in a sour mood, so I tried to cheer them up.

My teammates thanked me for being positive by pelting me with orange peels.

Back at home, I was nervous to tell Dad about the game.

151

I guess he seemed a little disappointed, but he got over it pretty quick.

But tonight, when Dad got home from dinner, he looked really mad. He plopped the newspaper down in front of me on the kitchen table, and here was the picture on the Sports page —

A "Blown" Opportunity

Red Socks goalie Gregory Heffley takes a break from the action as a fifty-yard kick by Demon Dawgs midfielder James Byron rolls in. The score ended the Socks' bid for an undefeated season.

Apparently, Dad found out about the paper from his boss at work.

GREAT SON YOU GOT THERE, FRANK!

OK, so maybe I didn't tell Dad ALL the details of the game.

In my defence, though, I didn't really know what happened until I read about it in the paper myself.

Dad didn't say a word to me for the rest of the night. If he's still mad at me, I just hope he gets over it pretty quick. Twisted Wizard 2 finally came out today, and I'm kind of counting on Dad to float me some money so I can get it.

Friday

Tonight after dinner, Dad took me and Rodrick out to a movie. It's not because he was trying to be nice, though. He just needed to get out of the house.

Remember how I told you that Mom got on an exercise kick a few months ago? Well, she quit after her first class. Dad took a picture of Mom decked out in all her exercise gear the first day she went to the gym, and tonight the pictures came in the mail.

The photo place gives you duplicate prints, so as a joke Dad wrote labels on the two pictures of Mom and put them up on the refrigerator.

Well, Dad was pretty proud of himself for coming up with that one, but Mom wasn't so amused.

Anyway, I guess Dad felt like maybe it was a good idea to put a little space between him and Mom tonight.

We went to the new movie theatre that just opened at the mall. After we bought our tickets, we went inside and gave them to the usher, who was a teenager with a crew cut. I didn't recognize him at first, but apparently Dad did.

YOUR TICKETS, SIR.

I read the teenager's name tag, and I couldn't believe my eyes. It was LENWOOD HEATH, the bad teenager who used to live on our street. The last I saw him, he had long hair and he was setting someone's trash on fire. But now here he was, looking like he just graduated from the air force or something.

Dad seemed REALLY impressed with Lenwood's new look, and the two of them struck up a conversation.

Lenwood said he's been going to Spag Union Military Academy, and he's just working at the movie theatre for spring break. Then Lenwood said he's trying to get good grades at Spag Union so he can get into West Point.

And all of a sudden Dad was treating Lenwood like his new best friend. Which was really crazy, especially considering the history between the two of them.

BEFORE   AFTER

Anyway, Dad kept chatting away with Lenwood, so me and Rodrick just got our popcorn and went in the theatre. And it wasn't until halfway through the movie that I realized what was REALLY happening.

If Dad saw how military school could make a man out of a juvenile delinquent like Lenwood Heath, then it wasn't a stretch to think it could make a man out of a wimp like ME.

I'm just praying Dad isn't having those thoughts. Right now I'm pretty concerned, because after the movie tonight, Dad was in the best mood I've seen him in for a LONG time.

<u>Monday</u>
Well, it's just like I feared. Dad spent the
whole weekend reading up on Spag Union, and
tonight he told me he's gonna sign me up.

Here's the worst part: "New recruits" have to
report on June 7th, when I'm supposed to be
on summer HOLIDAY.

Dad tried to convince me that this would be a
great thing for me, and how Spag Union would
really whip me into shape. But going off to boot
camp was NOT the way I was planning on
spending my school break.

I told Dad I won't last a DAY at Spag Union.
First of all, they mix kids my age in with
teenagers, and that can't be a good thing.

I'm sure the older kids would single me out on the first day.

But what I'm actually a lot more concerned with is the bathroom situation. I'll bet Spag Union is one of these places that has open showers with no stall doors, and that kind of set-up is not for me.

When it comes to the bathroom, I need my privacy. I don't even use the bathroom at school unless it's an absolute emergency.

A few classrooms in our school have bathrooms right in them, but I can't even use those, because every little sound you make is broadcasted to the whole room.

The only other option is to use the cafeteria bathroom, and that place is a complete madhouse. Somebody got the idea a few weeks ago to start throwing wet toilet paper around, so now that place is like a war zone.

I can't concentrate in that kind of an environment, so I basically have to hold it until I get home from school.

A couple of days ago, something happened that changed the situation. The janitor put some new air fresheners in the bathroom.

I started a rumour that the air fresheners were actually security cameras to catch whoever was throwing the wet toilet paper.

I guess I must've told the right people, because from that point on the cafeteria bathroom has been quieter than the library.

I might've solved the bathroom problem at
school, but I don't think I'm gonna be able to
pull off the same kind of trick at Spag Union.
And I SERIOUSLY doubt I can hold it for
the whole summer.

I knew I wasn't gonna convince Dad to change
his mind, so I went to Mom. I told her I didn't
want to go to a place where they make you shave
your head and do push-ups each day at 5:00
every morning. I figured she'd agree with me and
talk some sense into Dad.

But it looks like Mom isn't gonna be any help to me after all.

Wednesday

I knew I needed to do something quick to convince Dad that I was tough and didn't NEED to go to military academy. So I told him I wanted to join the Boy Scouts.

Dad seemed really enthusiastic about the idea, so that was a relief.

Besides trying to find a way to get Dad off my back, I have a couple of other reasons for wanting to join the Boy Scouts. Number one, Boy Scout meetings are on Sundays, so that means I can quit soccer.

And, number two, it's about time I start getting some respect from the other kids at school.

ATTENSHUN!

AS YOU WERE, GENTLEMEN!

There are actually TWO Boy Scout troops in my town: Troop 24, which is right in our neighbourhood, and Troop 133, which is about five miles down the road. Troop 133 is always having hot-dog roasts and pool parties and stuff like that, but Troop 24 is constantly out doing community-service projects on the weekends. So I'm definitely more of a Troop 133 kind of guy.

Now the trick is to make sure Dad doesn't find out about Troop 24, because he'll make me sign up with them for SURE.

In fact, tonight we were driving to the mall, and we passed Troop 24 cleaning up the park. Luckily, I distracted Dad at the last second.

Sunday

Today was my first Boy Scout meeting, and luckily it was with Troop 133. I got Rowley to sign up with me, too. When we got to the lodge, we met Mr Barrett, the Scoutmaster. He asked me and Rowley to say the Pledge of Allegiance and do a bunch of other stuff, and we were in. Mr Barrett even gave us our uniforms.

Rowley was happy because he thought the uniform was cool, but I was just happy to have a clean shirt for a change.

After we put our uniforms on, we joined the rest of the troop and started working on merit badges. Merit badges are these little patches you get for learning how to do all sorts of manly stuff.

Me and Rowley started flipping through the merit-badge book to see what we should work on.

Rowley wanted to do something hard like Wilderness Survival or Personal Fitness, but I talked him out of it. I said we should just start off with something nice and easy, so we settled on Whittling.

But whittling was a lot harder than I thought it would be. It took FOREVER to try to carve a block of wood into anything, and Rowley got a splinter within five minutes.

So we went to Mr Barrett and asked him if there was something less DANGEROUS we could do.

Mr Barrett said that if we were having trouble with the wood, maybe we could use soap instead. And that's when I knew I made the right call when I signed up with Troop 133.

Me and Rowley started carving the soap, but then I found out something really great. If you get the soap wet enough, you can just mould it into any shape you want with your hands. So we put away our whittling knives and SQUEEZED our soap into a shape instead.

My first creation was a sheep. I turned it in to Mr Barrett, and he checked one carving off my list.

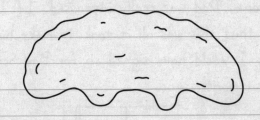

I didn't really know what to do for my next carving, so I just turned my sheep upside down and handed it back in as the Titanic.

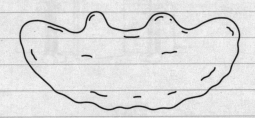

And, believe it or not, Mr Barrett accepted THAT one, too.

So me and Rowley both got our Whittling merit badges and pinned them to our uniforms. When I came home, Dad was really impressed. If I'd known that this was all it took to make him happy, I would have signed up for Boy Scouts about six months ago.

MAY

Sunday

The other day Mr Barrett announced that our Boy Scout troop was having a father-son campout this weekend, so I asked Dad if he'd go with me. I was pretty surprised with how easy it was to impress Dad with that one little merit badge, so I figured a whole WEEKEND of him seeing me do macho stuff would totally blow him away.

But yesterday morning I woke up as sick as a dog. I couldn't go, but Dad HAD to, because he signed up to be a driver.

I stayed in bed pretty much the whole day. I just wish I'd got sick on a WEEKDAY instead of a weekend. Last year I didn't miss any days of school, and I promised myself I wouldn't let THAT happen again.

The father-son camping trip turned out to be a DISASTER. The phone rang at 10:00 last night, and it was Dad calling from the emergency room.

Dad got put in a tent with the Woodley brothers, Darren and Marcus, because their dad couldn't come. Darren and Marcus were horsing around in the tent, even though Dad kept telling them to go to sleep. At one point Darren threw a football at Marcus, and it hit him in the stomach.

OOF!

Marcus wet his pants, and I guess Darren thought that was pretty funny.

Well, Marcus went totally BERSERK. He bit Darren, and he wouldn't let go, either.

It took Dad a long time to prise the two of them apart, and he had to take Darren to the emergency room after that.

Dad came home this morning, and he was not real happy with ME for getting him stuck in that situation. Something tells me that after this weekend he's not a big fan of Troop 133, either.

Sunday
Today was Mother's Day, and I didn't have anything to give to Mom.

I was going to ask Dad to take me to the store so I could at least get Mom a card or something, but Dad was still recovering from the father-son campout. And I don't think he was looking to do me any favours, anyway.

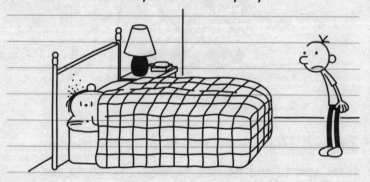

So I had to come up with a homemade gift.

Last year I made Mom a "Chore Coupon" book for Mother's Day. Each coupon had something like "One free lawn mowing" or "One free window washing" on it.

One free car wash

I give Dad a Chore Coupon book just about every Father's Day, and it always works out great. It's a way for me to take care of my gift obligation without having to spend any money, and Dad never actually uses any of his coupons in the book.

HUH? OH, UM, THANKS.

Mom cashed in every single ONE of HER coupons last year. So I didn't want to make the same mistake this year.

I tried to think of something original to make for Mom today, but I ran out of time. So I ended up just piggybacking on Manny's gift.

<u>Monday</u>

I figure the best way to get Dad to forget that father-son camping mess is to make it up to him. So tonight at dinner I asked Dad if he wanted to go on a camping trip, just me and him.

I've been studying up on my Boy Scouts manual, and I'm pretty eager to show off what I've learned.

Well, Dad didn't exactly jump at my offer, but Mom thought it was a GREAT idea. She said we should go this weekend and that Rodrick could go, too. She said it would be a great "bonding" experience for the three of us.

I wasn't too enthusiastic about that idea, and neither was Rodrick.

In fact, one of the reasons I wanted to get out of the house this weekend is because me and Rodrick are in a fight.

Last night Mom was giving Rodrick a haircut in the kitchen. Usually when Mom gives us boys a haircut, she puts a towel round our necks so the hair doesn't get all over our clothes. But yesterday Mom used one of her old maternity dresses instead of a towel. So when I saw Rodrick like that, I knew I had to take advantage of the situation.

FLASH SNIP

I ran upstairs and locked myself in the bathroom before Rodrick had a chance to catch me and take the camera. And I didn't come back out until I was sure he was gone.

Rodrick got me back, anyway. Last night I had a nightmare that I was sleeping on a nest of red ants, and that was thanks to him.

The way I see it, now we're even. But if there's one thing I've learned about Rodrick it's that he's still not gonna let it go. So that's why I'm not that eager to hole up in a tent with him for the weekend.

Saturday
Today me, Dad and Rodrick headed off on our camping trip. I picked a place that had a lot of manly activities that you could do.

179

On the way to the campground, the sky got dark, and then it started to rain.

I wasn't all that concerned, because our tent is waterproof, and Mom packed ponchos for everybody. But, by the time we got to our campsite, it was six inches underwater.

We were pretty far from home, so Dad decided we should just find a place to stay for the night.

I was really bummed, because the whole point of the trip was for me to impress Dad with my camping skills, and now we were just gonna stay in some stupid hotel room.

Dad found a place and got a room with two beds and a pullout couch. We watched TV for a while and then started getting ready for bed.

First, Dad went downstairs to the front desk to complain that the heater was too loud, so I was alone in the room with Rodrick.

I went into the bathroom to brush my teeth, and when I came out Rodrick was looking out of the peephole. Then he said something that made me freeze in my tracks.

He said that Holly Hills and her family were out in the hallway, and they were staying in the room right ACROSS from us.

I had to see this for myself. So I moved him out of the way and looked out of the peephole.

The hallway was completely empty. And before I realized it was a trick Rodrick gave me a big shove, and I fell out of the door.

Then it got WORSE. Rodrick locked the door behind me, and I was stuck in the hallway wearing nothing but my tighty whities.

I pounded on the door, but Rodrick wouldn't let me back in the room.

I was making a big racket, and I realized people in the nearby rooms were gonna start opening their doors to find out what was going on. So I ran round the corner to save myself the embarrassment of anyone seeing me. I spent about fifteen minutes sneaking through the hallways, hiding every time I heard voices.

I was gonna go back to our room and beg Rodrick to let me in, but then I realized I didn't even know our ROOM number. And all the doors looked exactly the same to me.

I couldn't exactly go down to the front desk, either. The only option I really had was to try to find Dad.

Then I remembered: Dad is a junk-food addict. I knew he'd eventually turn up at the vending machines, so that's where I camped out.

I wedged myself in between the soda machine and the candy machine and waited. I had to wait a really long time, but Dad finally did show up.

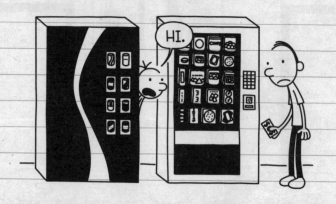

You know what, though? After seeing the look on Dad's face, I kind of wished I'd just sucked it up and gone to the front desk instead.

Sunday

Well, after our camping trip, I'm pretty sure there's no chance I can convince Dad to change his mind about Spag Union. So, at this point, I'm not even gonna bother trying.

I realized there are only about three more weeks before I get shipped out, so I figure this is my last chance to make a play for Holly Hills. If I'm lucky, maybe I can take some good memories with me to military academy, and my summer won't be so bad.

185

I've been working up the nerve to talk to Holly for a long time, and I decided it was now or never.

When we went to church today, I tried to make sure we sat right near the Hills family. But we ended up two rows in front of them, which I guess was close enough. And during the part where everybody shakes hands with one another I made my move.

The hand-shaking thing was actually just step one in a two-part plan, and the second part would come tonight. My next step was to call Holly on the phone and use the hand-shaking thing to get the conversation started.

At dinner tonight, I told everyone that I needed to make a very important call, so everyone should stay off the phone. But I guess Rodrick must've figured out I was gonna call a girl, because he took all the handsets and hid them.

That meant the only way to make a call was to use the speakerphone in the kitchen, but there was no chance of THAT happening.

I told Mom that Rodrick took all the phones, and she made him return them to where they belonged.

Eventually, Rodrick went down to the basement. Later on I snuck into Mom and Dad's room to make my call. I turned off the lights so Rodrick wouldn't know I was in there, and I hid under a blanket. Then I waited for about twenty minutes to make sure he hadn't followed me.

Before I had a chance to dial Holly's number, someone walked in the room and turned on the light. I thought for SURE it was Rodrick.

But it wasn't. It was DAD.

CLICK

I decided to stay perfectly still and let Dad
get whatever he needed and leave.

But Dad didn't leave. He got into bed and started
reading a BOOK.

I should have just uncovered myself the second
Dad walked in the room, because now I couldn't
just get up and walk out or I'd give him a heart
attack. So I decided to just sneak out of the
room real slow.

I moved about an inch a second. I figured it
would take me about a half hour to make it all
the way out of the room, but there would still be
enough time to call Holly after that.

I was only about five inches from the bedroom door when the phone in my hand rang and scared the living daylights out of me.

I think Dad really DID almost have a heart attack. And, once he recovered, he didn't look happy to see me.

Dad made me get out of his room, and then he slammed the door.

I'm sure this episode didn't help my standing with Dad, but I guess at this point it's probably too late, anyway.

Tuesday

Two days have already passed since I shook
hands with Holly, and I didn't want any more
time to go by before I spoke with her again.

Luckily, Dad and Rodrick weren't home tonight,
so I knew I could make a phone call without
being bothered. I practised what I was going to
say about a million times, and then I finally
worked up the nerve to make the call.

I dialled Holly's number, and the phone started
ringing. But right then Mom picked up the
phone downstairs.

Mom has this REALLY bad habit of just dialling
without checking to see if anyone else is using
the phone, and that's what she did tonight.

I tried to stop her, but it was no use.

The phone kept ringing at the Hills's house, and then someone picked up. It was Holly's mother.

Mom was really confused, since she didn't dial the Hills's number in the first place. I just held my breath and waited for it all to be over.

It took Mom and Mrs Hills a minute to figure out who was on the other end of the line. But, once they did, they just started chatting like nothing strange had happened at all.

They got into this long conversation about the PTA and the fundraising committee and stuff like that. I couldn't really hang up, because then Mom would hear the click and know someone was on the other end.

Eventually, the conversation between Mom and Mrs Hills turned to me.

...CALLED HIS BROTHER A "PLOOPY". MM HMM...

At that point I just put the phone down and went to bed. I figure that a phone call between me and Holly isn't meant to be, so I'm officially giving up.

Friday

Today at school I overheard Holly tell a couple of her friends that she was gonna meet them at the rollerskating rink tonight, and a lightbulb went on over my head.

After school I asked Mom if she'd take me to the Roll-a-Round tonight, and she said yes but I'd have to get a ride home from someone else's parents. So I invited Rowley along.

As soon as Rowley showed up at my front door, I knew I'd made a mistake inviting him.

Rowley had his hair all teased up, and he was dressed just like his favourite singer, Joshie.

And I think Rowley might have even been wearing sparkly lip gloss, but I can't say for sure. I couldn't stop to worry about the way Rowley looked, though, because I had my OWN problems. Earlier on I had lost one of my contact lenses, so that meant I had to wear my back-up glasses. The lenses on those things are about three inches thick, and they look RIDICULOUS.

If I'm not wearing my contact lenses or my glasses, I'm as blind as a bat. I guess I should just feel lucky that I wasn't alive during caveman times, because I wouldn't have been able to hunt or do anything useful. I'm sure my tribe-mates would've ditched me the first chance they got.

I probably would've had to become a wise man or something just to make everyone think I was worth keeping around.

On the ride to the rollerskating rink tonight, I gave Rowley some instructions on how to behave if I got into a conversation with Holly Hills - knowing him, he could seriously hurt my chances with her.

I wish I had waited until we were out of the car, because Mom overheard our conversation.

HOLLY HILLS? HOLLY HILLS WAS THE ONLY FOUR-YEAR-OLD AT PRE-SCHOOL WHO WASN'T POTTY TRAINED.

LA LA LA... I CAN'T HEAR YOU!

When we pulled up at the Roll-a-Round, I got out of the car before Mom could say anything ELSE I didn't want to hear.

Me and Rowley paid our admission and then went inside. We rented our skates and brought them over to the arcade area, where I scoped out the whole scene.

I spotted Holly over by the snack bar. She was with a bunch of her friends, so I wasn't ready to go and talk to her just yet.

At 9:00 the DJ announced "Couples Skate". A lot of people were pairing up, and Holly was sitting at a table, all alone. I knew this was the chance I was waiting for.

I started making my way over to her, but getting around on skates was a LOT harder than I thought it would be. I had to hug the wall just to stay on my feet.

It was taking FOREVER, and I realized the song was gonna be over by the time I got to Holly. So I got down on my butt and scooted over to her to speed things up.

SCOOCH
SCOOCH

I almost got run over a couple of times, but I finally made it to the snack bar.

Holly was still there, sitting by herself. Time was running out, so I had to take a shortcut through a puddle of soda to get to her.

On my way across the snack bar, I tried to work out what I was going to say to Holly. I realized I wasn't looking my coolest at that moment, so I knew I was gonna have to say something pretty smooth to make up for it. But before I even had a chance to open my mouth, Holly said four words that changed everything —

I started to tell her I was Greg Heffley, the guy from the "Doggie Dropped It" joke, but right then Couples Skate ended, and Holly's friends swooped in and pulled her out on to the rink.

I made my way back to the arcade, and that's where I stayed for the rest of the night. Because, believe me, I was NOT in the mood for skating.

CAN I GO GET A SODA?

NO.

You know, I probably should've realized a long time ago that Holly wasn't worth my time. Somebody who would mistake ME for FREGLEY definitely has something wrong with them.

I'm officially DONE with girls. I should just ask Dad to see if Spag Union has early admission, because there's really no point in me sticking around here any more.

JUNE

Friday
Today was the last day of school, and everybody was in a good mood but me. Everyone ELSE is looking forward to having fun this summer, but all I've got to look forward to is sit-ups and marching drills.

At lunch, everyone handed their yearbooks around for people to sign, and when I got mine back, here's what was on the last page –

At first I couldn't figure out who "Slick" was, but then I realized it was just Rowley. A couple of days ago, Rowley was standing near an older kid's locker, and the guy wanted Rowley to move.

So here's what the guy said –

So I guess now Rowley thinks "Slick" is his permanent nickname or something. I just hope he doesn't expect ME to say it.

I flipped through the pages to see who else signed my yearbook, and there was one that made me stop in my tracks. It was from Holly Hills.

First of all, she wrote my actual name, so that means she figured out who I was since Friday night. And, second, she wrote "K.I.T." at the end, which everyone knows means "Keep in Touch". You'd better BELIEVE I'm gonna take her up on her offer.

Greg,

I don't really know you all that well, but you seem OK, I guess.

K.I.T.
Holly

I handed my yearbook to Rowley to show him what Holly wrote. But then he showed me what she wrote in HIS yearbook, and it kind of made her note to me look lame.

Dear Rowley,
You are so adorable & funny! I hope we have the same homeroom next year. Stay cute!

Love, Holly

A couple of minutes later, Holly's yearbook came around, and I had a chance to sign it. So here's what I put –

Dear Holly–

You are a nice person and all, but I only think of you as a friend.

From,

Slick

The way I see it, I just did Rowley a HUGE favour. I don't want his heart stomped on by Holly Hills, because the truth is girls can be a little cruel sometimes.

Saturday
Today was my only day of summer holiday, and I had to spend it at Seth Snella's half-birthday party. I asked Mom to let me stay home so I could enjoy myself, but she said we were going to the party as a family.

Dad didn't even bother fighting it, because he knew HE wasn't getting out of it, either.

So at 1:00 we walked across the street to the Snellas' house.

The Snellas really did it up this year. They had a clown making balloon animals, and a bouncy castle for the kids.

They even had live music. Rodrick was pretty sore over that because his band, Löded Diper, tried out for the job, but the Snellas turned them down.

Everyone ate lunch, and then at 3:30 the main event started.

Mr and Mrs Snella had all the adults line up in front of Seth, and they all took turns trying to make him smile. Mr Henrich went first.

SQUAWK!
SQUAWK!

I noticed Dad looking really nervous at the back of the line. At one point I walked by Dad to get myself some cupcakes, and he stopped me. He told me if I could get him out of this situation, he'd owe me BIG-time.

I thought it was pretty ironic that Dad would be asking ME for a favour, especially since he's the one who's shipping me off to military school tomorrow. So I was fine with letting him squirm.

But that doesn't mean I wanted to see my Dad acting like a baboon in front of the whole neighbourhood, either. I thought about sneaking home to spare myself the shame.

That's when I saw Manny on the other side of the deck, poking around Seth's presents.

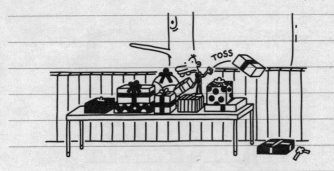

Manny found the present that was from OUR family, and he ripped it open. As soon as I saw what it was, I knew things were about to get real complicated.

It was a blue knitted blanket, just like the one MANNY used to have as a baby. And you could tell Manny thought he had found himself a brand-new Tingy.

I went over to Manny and told him he was gonna have to hand over the blanket because it was for the baby, not him. But Manny wouldn't cough it up.

When Manny realized I was gonna take away the blanket, he just turned round and chucked it over the railing.

The blanket landed in the branch of a tree. I knew I had to get it back before Mom found out, so I got down off the deck and started climbing up the tree.

Right when I was about to grab the blanket, my foot slipped, and I was left hanging there. I tried to pull myself back up, but I didn't have the strength.

I probably would've been able to do it, but the only thing I'd had to eat today was a grape soda and the frosting off a piece of cake, so I had no energy.

I yelled for help, but I really wish I hadn't called attention to myself. Because right when everyone came over to see what was going on, my trousers came loose and fell down round my ankles.

It wouldn't have happened if I was wearing my OWN trousers. But I never washed my smart trousers after they got that chocolate all over them, so I was borrowing a pair of RODRICK's trousers, which were about two sizes too big for me.

The situation was humiliating enough, but then I realized something even WORSE. I was wearing my Wonder Woman Underoos.

Eventually, Dad ran over and helped get me down, but not before Mr Snella got the whole thing on tape. And something tells me that this time round he has a good shot at the "America's Funniest Families" Grand Prize.

After that, Dad hustled me home, and I thought he was gonna be really mad at me. But it turns out that my accident happened right when Dad was next up to go in front of Seth Snella, so I saved him from having to take his turn.

And get this: Dad thinks I FAKED the whole thing to bail him out.

I wasn't about to correct him, either. I made myself a big bowl of ice cream, sat down in front of the TV and tried to enjoy the rest of my one day of freedom as best I could.

Sunday

When I woke up this morning, it was a quarter past 11:00. I couldn't figure out why I was still in bed, because Dad was supposed to drive me to Spag Union at 8:00.

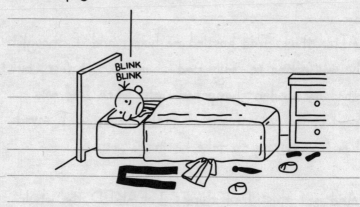

So I went downstairs. Dad was sitting at the kitchen table reading the paper, and he wasn't even dressed yet.

When I walked into the kitchen, Dad told me we could "rethink" this military academy thing. He said maybe I could just do some push-ups and sit-ups every once in a while, and that would be just as good as the summer conditioning programme at Spag Union.

I couldn't believe my ears. I guess Dad felt like he owed me for saving him yesterday, and this was his way of paying me back.

I walked out of the house and went up to Rowley's before Dad could change his mind. And on my way up the hill, I realized that I was on summer holiday.

I knocked on Rowley's door, and when he answered I told him I didn't have to go to Spag Union AFTER all.

Rowley didn't even know what I was talking about, so that just shows you how clueless he can be sometimes.

We played Rowley's Twisted Wizard 2 for a while, and then his parents kicked us out of the house. So we grabbed some popsicles and went and sat on his front kerb.

You'll never BELIEVE what happened next. A really cute girl I had never seen before walked up to us and introduced herself.

214

She said her name was Trista and that she just
moved in down the street.

I looked at Rowley, and it was pretty obvious he
was thinking what I was thinking. So it took me
about two seconds to come up with a plan.

But then I had a BETTER idea.

Rowley's family belongs to a country club, and he's allowed to bring two guests to his pool every day.

So that could actually work out real nice.

It looks like things are finally going my way and, you know, it's about time. I don't know anyone who deserves to catch a break more than me, because, like I said before, I'm pretty much one of the best people I know.

And I know it's really corny to finish with a happy ending, but it looks like I'm out of paper anyway, so I guess this is

THE END.

ACKNOWLEDGEMENTS

Thanks to my wife, Julie, without whose love and support these books would not be possible. Thanks to my family – Mom, Dad, Re, Scott and Pat – and to my extended family – the Kinneys, Cullinanes, Johnsons, Fitchs, Kennedys and Burdetts. You have all been so supportive of this endeavour, and it has been great fun to share this experience with you!

Thanks, as always, to my editor, Charlie Kochman, for taking a chance on this series; to Jason Wells, the best publicity director in the business; and to all of the great folks at Abrams.

Thanks to my boss, Jess Brallier, and to all of my co-workers at Family Education Network.

Thanks to Riley, Sylvie, Carla, Nina, Brad, Elizabeth and Keith out in Hollywoodland.

Thanks to Mel Odom for his wonderfully bombastic write-ups of the first two books.

And thanks to Aaron Nicodemus for encouraging me Way Back When to pick up my cartooning pen after I had given up.

ABOUT THE AUTHOR

Jeff Kinney is the creator of Poptropica.com, and the author of the #1 *New York Times* bestsellers *Diary of a Wimpy Kid* and *Diary of a Wimpy Kid: Rodrick Rules*, as well as the *Diary of a Wimpy Kid Do-It-Yourself Book*. He spent his childhood in the Washington, D.C., area and moved to New England in 1995. Jeff lives in southern Massachusetts with his wife, Julie, and their two sons, Will and Grant.